Maisie
Hitchins

To all the brilliant readers who have told me how much they loved Maisie – this last adventure is for you!
~HW

For Lucy and for Elizabeth
~ML

STRIPES PUBLISHING LIMITED
An imprint of the Little Tiger Group
1 Coda Studios, 189 Munster Road,
London SW6 6AW

A paperback original
First published in Great Britain in 2015

ISBN: 978-1-84715-597-9

A CIP catalogue record for this book is available from the British Library.

Printed and bound in the UK.

468109753

Holly Webb Illustrated by Marion Lindsay

Maisie Hitchins

The Case of the Weeping Mermaid

STRIPES

31 Albion Street, London

Attic:
Maisie's grandmother and Sally the maid

Third floor:
Miss Lane's rooms

Second floor:
Mr Smith's rooms

First floor:
Professor Tobin's rooms

Ground floor:
Entrance hall, sitting room and dining room

Basement:
Maisie's room, kitchen and yard entrance

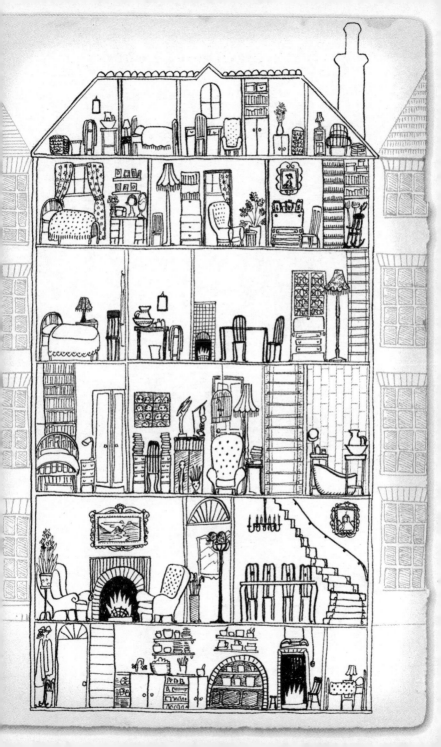

"Come on, Eddie!" Maisie hurried across the pretty square, eager to get to Alice's house. Now that Alice was home from her smart boarding school, Maisie had hoped she would see her best friend more often. But it seemed like ages since they'd had a proper talk, and Maisie didn't have all that long before Gran would want her back home to help with supper. She scurried up the steps to the house and banged the shiny brass knocker. Eddie sat down on the top step looking exhausted, even though Maisie had carried him for part of the way.

"Good afternoon, Miss."

Maisie blinked in surprise – it wasn't the smart parlourmaid she'd expected who had opened the front door. Alice's family had more servants than they knew what to do with, but this harassed-looking girl had been just a housemaid the last time she'd visited.

Perhaps Elizabeth is having her afternoon off, Maisie thought. She was rather glad – the parlourmaid always looked down her nose at Maisie with her faded dress and small, rather scruffy dog peering round her ankles.

"I've come to see Miss Alice. She should be—" Maisie started to say, but the girl just nodded and stood back from the door.

"She's in the garden, Miss, playing in her tree house. You're best off going out through here." She waved Maisie into a small parlour, its French windows standing open, and then hurried away.

Maisie stared after her. It felt as though something rather odd was going on. "This way, Eddie," she murmured, and they took the path down the garden to the giant tree where Alice had her beautiful little house. It had been a present from her father. It sat in the crook of the branches, quite high up, with its polished windows glinting in the sunlight. Alice cleaned the tree house herself – it was the only housework she ever had to do.

Maisie sighed as she began to climb the wooden staircase that wound around the tree trunk. Gran had said that she could come to visit Alice, but Maisie knew quite well that she'd have to make up for lost time when she got back to 31 Albion Street. Gran was probably making a long list of jobs this minute.

Still, Maisie had a good hour before she had to worry about that. She hurried up the last few steps calling, "Alice! Alice!"

The door flew open and Alice bounced out, dragging Maisie into the tree house and hurrying her into one of the pretty flowered armchairs by the window. "Oh, Maisie, it's been weeks since I've seen you!" she said, handing both Maisie and Eddie a biscuit, then sitting down and beaming.

"I suppose it is a fortnight," Maisie agreed. "Are you all right, Alice?" she asked, a little worriedly. Alice looked pale and, even though she was smiling, there was a frown line running from her forehead to her nose.

Alice sighed. "You'll think I'm being silly." She glanced sideways at Maisie and then looked down again hurriedly.

"I promise I won't." Maisie reached out to take Alice's hand. Her friend's nails were bitten, she noticed in surprise. Alice *never* bit her nails. She was always so very neat and tidy.

"Really, what's the matter?" Maisie asked again.

Alice let out a huge sigh. "It's Papa. He's behaving so strangely. It started not long after he and my stepmama came home from their honeymoon. He was blissfully happy – they both were. But now he looks anxious all the time. I'm sure he's got thinner and he hardly talks to me at all. He's always rushing in and out, going to meetings. And it's not that he and Mama have discovered they don't like each other after all, or anything like that. Mama looks worried, too, a lot of the time. But they won't tell me why! Whenever I ask, they say it's nothing and that I'm just imagining it, but I'm not, Maisie, I'm really not." Alice stopped, took a deep breath, and stared at her friend. "I'm so glad you're here. If you hadn't visited today, I think I might have come to you and asked you to investigate. I'm absolutely convinced that something strange is going on. It's a mystery."

Maisie spent the rest of her visit trying to calm Alice down and promising her that of course she would investigate if Alice wanted her to. But she didn't really believe that there was anything wrong. Mr Lacey was so nice, and so sensible, and he was very, very rich. Why would he be involved in a mystery? Maisie was almost sure that Alice was making something out of nothing.

But as Alice was escorting her and Eddie back to the front door (she had very ladylike manners), she suddenly stopped and clutched

Maisie's arm so hard Maisie nearly squeaked.

"What is it?"

"Papa! That's his study, I can hear him walking over to the door!" Alice nodded towards the door in the dark panelling and hauled Maisie backwards, so it looked as though they were just walking into the hallway. It would appear that they'd run into her father by chance.

Sure enough, the study door opened, and Mr Lacey came out into the hall as the girls walked past.

"Oh, Papa! Maisie came to visit," Alice said, rather fast.

Her father didn't seem to notice the odd tone in her voice. He nodded politely and smiled at Maisie, but he looked distracted.

"Could you tell your mama I won't be in for dinner, Alice dear?" he murmured.

"I must go down to the office…" Then he kissed his daughter, seized his hat from a little table by the door and hurried out without even putting on a coat.

"You see?" Alice muttered, as the door slammed behind him.

Maisie nodded. Mr Lacey hadn't seemed quite himself, she could see what Alice meant. And, now she thought about it, there had been an odd smell as he leaned over to kiss Alice goodbye.

"Tea!" Maisie said suddenly. "I've never noticed him smelling of tea before."

"It's from the warehouse at the docks," Alice said sadly. "He's there all the time! A lot of his ships are importing tea. It's very … very… Oh, you know what I mean, it makes a lot of money. Tea, and beautiful china, and silks and tobacco – lots of things." She waved at a table full of exotic-looking china just inside the door of the drawing room. Maisie had already noticed it – her gran loved pretty china, and she'd been thinking how much Gran would admire the pattern with its sprays of fanciful flowers, all edged in gold. "Please tell me you'll investigate, Maisie. I'm sure that something is terribly wrong."

Maisie was still thinking about Mr Lacey's strange behaviour as she walked past 31 Albion Street – she was planning to enter through the back door in the yard. She was so preoccupied that she didn't notice the carrier's cart pulling up behind her. She only turned round when a boy yelled, "Oy! Ginger!"

"What?" Maisie snapped at him. She hated it when people made comments about her red hair.

"Got a parcel for you. Maisie Hitchins, right?

You're popular. Brought you a parcel a couple of weeks back, didn't I?"

"Oh." Maisie nodded. She couldn't be rude to him if he was delivering a parcel – and she didn't care if the boy made comments about her hair now, anyway. It had to be another package from her father!

Daniel Hitchins was first mate on a merchant navy vessel, and Maisie hadn't seen him since she was very little. But now he was on his way home – slowly. His ship was taking a roundabout sort of route and had to call at various ports on the way, so his presents came home before he did. The last time she had heard from him, he had been in Egypt.

"Thank you!" she called, waving to the boy as she dashed into the alleyway and round to the back door. "Gran! Gran! A parcel!"

Her gran was sitting at the kitchen table with one of their lodgers, Mr Smith. Strictly speaking, lodgers weren't supposed to sit in the kitchen, but Mr Smith was a special case. He was a sailor, too – in fact, he had sailed with Maisie's father, as ship's cook. He was retired now, but Maisie thought he missed the sea. He missed cooking, too, and somehow he'd persuaded Gran that she needed his help in the kitchen. Maisie certainly wasn't complaining. Mr Smith peeled potatoes faster than anyone she had ever seen – even though he only had one working eye. The other eye had been replaced with a bright blue glass one, which rolled around in a most disturbing manner. Now he looked curiously at the parcel, eyeing the string and sealing wax.

"From your dad, is it?" he asked wistfully.

"I think so," Maisie nodded eagerly.

Mr Smith passed her his clasp knife to cut the string. She undid the layers of brown paper, and brought out a letter and a beautiful wooden box, so smooth it felt like silk, with brass corners and a brass lock

that was engraved with fantastical dragons.
Maisie stroked it admiringly and turned
the key. It opened with a well oiled click,
revealing a parcel of papers, tied up with
more string and sealing wax.

"Whatever's all that?" Gran asked curiously. "You'd better read his letter, Maisie."

Maisie nodded and unfolded the closely written sheet.

Dearest Maisie,

Just a short note before I send this off to you. Tell your gran I am on my way home, not too far away now. I bought this box months ago when we were at Pekin, China, and I have been using it to keep all my papers in. Just letters and such, if anyone asks. But that's not quite true. I want you to keep them safe, Maisie. Don't let anyone read them but you. Something strange has been going on, something I first noticed while we were in China. Strange and worrying, and I've been puzzling over it ever since. Perhaps your sharp eyes will catch something I haven't. Think it over for me, Maisie, and I shall see you soon.

From your loving father,
Daniel Hitchins

Maisie blinked down at the note. "It's just some old letters," she murmured. "He says to keep them safe for him, that's all."

She could feel her cheeks reddening, partly with keeping a secret from Gran and Mr Smith, but also with delight. She ran her fingers over the engraved eye pattern on her carnelian pendant. Her father had sent her another special mystery to solve!

That night, Maisie curled up in her bed
with Eddie close by her on the rug. She was
weary – there had been a lot of housework
to do after her visit to Alice's, and she felt
as though she had been running around
all day. But even though a little bit of her
longed to snuggle up under her patchwork
quilt and sleep, the rest of her was wide
awake and eager to look at the letters in her
precious box.

There were several sheets of loose paper,
she realized, as she lifted them out and
untied the string. But most of the pile was
actually a battered old notebook with limp
cardboard covers, much worn and stained.

Maisie opened it carefully and began to
flick through the pages. Her father seemed
to have used it as a sort of memory book. He
had stuck in postcards and strange-looking

faded flowers. There were little sketches of his shipmates, too, and they made Maisie giggle – all of them seemed to be very odd-looking.

After a few pages, the book became more serious. The notes seemed to be set down more carefully, as if the subject was more important.

September 14th

Another ship lost. <u>Belle of Arcady</u>. And so soon after the <u>Sarah-Rose</u>. Am beginning to have suspicions.

Most valuable cargo. Ivory and tea. Someone could make a lot of money selling that off on the sly.

Or it could be the ship owners themselves, claiming on the insurance. Report the ship as lost, and just repaint her and rename her. Happens more than you might think.

But is it happening here? Perhaps am just too suspicious for my own good.

Maisie turned over the pages eagerly,
flicking past more postcards and a fragment
of a poem. Ah! Here was more about the
case.

October 2nd

Almost sure now that there is some
sort of swindle going on. I heard that
the Lily May was lost with all hands
two years ago, but I swear I have
just seen her again. That mermaid
figurehead, I'd know it anywhere. I
was a cabin boy on the Lily May, she
was my first ship! Old Captain Jones
liked his mermaid to be perfect - I
must have touched up that paintwork
whenever we put in at a port. I'll
always remember her - the way the
drops of resin seeping from the wood

made her look as if she were crying.
Surely there couldn't be another the
same?

Maisie sucked in her breath excitedly.
A clue, a real clue! The notebook was
fascinating. Maisie didn't know what all her
father's sailor talk meant – he kept mentioning
the strangest things: reefs and tackles,
Andrews and barks. A lot of it didn't make
sense. But she thought she understood the
mystery he was trying to solve. Someone had
been making ships disappear. They would be
claimed as lost at sea, and then the thieves
could sell off the cargo and sail the ship away
to be repainted and renamed. The crew would
have to be in on the crime as well, of course,
Maisie thought, frowning to herself. Or else
they'd have to be sacked before the ship was

"lost". She shuddered. Sacked, or perhaps just got rid of. Permanently. It would be more realistic, wouldn't it, if some sailors went down with the ship?

Her father had drawn a sketch of the figurehead under his notes – a beautiful wooden statue of a girl, staring out from the very front of the ship, just under the bow. She was carved with long, waving hair and tears on her cheeks, and Maisie could see the beginnings of her mermaid tail, before she merged into the wooden boards of the ship itself.

Maisie was sure her father was right – he couldn't have made a mistake. And she was convinced that with his description and the drawing, she would recognize the weeping mermaid herself.

Chapter Two

Maisie was polishing the wooden banisters of the stairs up to the first floor, when the doorbell rang. It pealed on and on, and then the person at the front door began to bang the knocker, too. Eddie, who had been sleeping curled up on the landing, jumped up and began to bark as if it were burglars. Maisie could hear Professor Tobin, who had the first-floor rooms, muttering. "Oh, dash it!"

The professor wasn't usually grumpy, but Maisie suspected that the noise might have made him jump and upset his bottle of ink. It was probably all over his papers. And his desk and the carpet. She sighed and galloped down the stairs to open the door, before whoever was there broke the knocker clean off.

"Alice!" Maisie was quite astonished. For a start, Alice was there all by herself, without her stepmother or a maid. There was a hansom cab just pulling away from the pavement – Alice had come in a cab, all on her own! And Maisie simply couldn't believe that it had been Alice making all that noise. Her friend was always so very polite.

"What on earth's the matter?" Maisie demanded, taking in Alice's reddened cheeks and glittering eyes.

"Oh, Maisie, I'm sorry to turn up out of the blue like this," Alice said, her words tumbling over each other as she hurried into the hallway. "I simply had to come and see you." She stopped all at once, and then swallowed. When she spoke again, her voice was squeaky and breathless. "I've come to say goodbye."

"What?" Maisie stared at her. "Whatever do you mean?"

"We're leaving." Alice sat down suddenly on the bottom step of the stairs. "We're going to China," she told Maisie. She sounded as though she didn't quite believe it herself.

"You can't be!" Maisie shook her head. "Alice, that's the other side of the world. You can't go there!"

"We have to," Alice sighed.

Maisie sat down on the step next to her friend and put an arm round her.

"Why?" Maisie murmured.

"Papa's business. I've found out why he's been looking so worried. Three of his ships have foundered, Maisie – that means they were lost at sea. It's terribly sad, of course. The men aboard must have drowned. And it means that all the cargo was lost, the tea, and silks and things. The ships are expensive to build, too." She was silent for a minute, and then she added, "Altogether, it means that Papa has lost an awful lot of money. He is … almost ruined."

Maisie nodded slowly. Alice's father was very rich, and Alice had only ever been a rich man's daughter. Maisie had a feeling that Alice didn't know how to be poor.

"That's dreadful. Oh, Alice, I'm so sorry. But I don't understand. Why does that mean you have to go to China?"

"All three of the ships disappeared close to Chinese ports," Alice explained. "Papa wishes to try to find out what has happened. He suspects that perhaps they were sunk on purpose. He says that maybe he has made an enemy who sank the ships for revenge!"

Maisie stared at Alice doubtfully. She couldn't imagine calm, sensible Mr Lacey saying anything so dramatic. But at the same time, the story reminded Maisie of what she'd read in her father's notebook. Who could have thought that the shipping trade was so dangerous?

Alice frowned. "It does seem like something out of one of those Penny Dreadful magazines that your friend George reads. But honestly, Maisie, Papa did say that, and he sounded awful. He's told me before that some of the other people in the shipping business are terrible cut-throats, but I never thought he meant it quite like that." She leaned her head on Maisie's shoulder. "Our house is to be let out to strangers," she murmured. "I wonder who will sleep in my room? Oh, I do hope they'll look after my lovely tree house…"

She looked so pale and sad that Maisie pulled her up and marched her across the hallway to the back stairs. "You need a cup of tea," she said firmly. "You look like you're about to keel over."

Maisie steered Alice down the stairs and into the little passageway that led to the kitchen and scullery, and her tiny bedroom. As Maisie led her friend into the kitchen, Mr Smith jumped up, dropping the peeling knife.

"Good gracious! Miss Alice!" Gran turned round from the stove to stare. "Whatever's the matter with you, child? You're as white as skimmed milk. Here, Maisie, sit her down."

"She's upset, Gran. She's got to go away." Maisie explained about China and the lost ships, while Gran and Mr Smith stared at Alice, and Alice stared at her hands in her lap.

"Oh dear. Oh dear me," Gran murmured, when Maisie had finished. "That's a terrible thing. China! Such a long way away…"

"It isn't right," Mr Smith muttered suddenly. He had been silent all the way through Maisie's story, and now both girls jumped when he spoke. "Not right to take such a little thing all that way. Look at her. She's not made for the sun."

Maisie eyed Alice. She understood what Mr Smith meant. Her friend was always pale, even when she wasn't miserable, and she had been thin and delicate-looking ever since she had been ill a few months before.

"Nor for a long sea voyage either," Mr Smith added, shaking his head. "It's just not right."

"My stepmama said the same thing,"

Alice told him, looking up at last. "She said it wasn't a healthy place to take a young lady. But then she hugged me and said that perhaps we would grow used to the heat after all and she was going to take the most special care of me."

"Why don't you—?" Maisie started to ask, and then she stopped. She had been going to ask why Alice didn't just go back to Miss Prenderby's Academy for Young Ladies, the boarding school that she had attended while her father and stepmother went on their wedding trip. Even though there had been a spate of thefts while Alice was at the school, and one particularly horrible girl who had bullied everyone, Maisie knew that Alice had enjoyed being there. It had been so different from her quiet life at home with a governess.

But just as Maisie had started to say it,

she had remembered that Miss Prenderby's was probably dreadfully expensive. Several of the young ladies were the daughters of lords, after all, and there had once been a girl at the school who was almost a princess, or would have been if several cousins had obligingly died.

Maisie frowned and went on. "Why don't you come and stay with us?" Then she looked up at Gran guiltily. It wasn't really up to her to invite people to stay. And Alice's parents might not be able to pay much for lodging now. Besides, they didn't have any rooms free.

But Gran was nodding. "She'd have to share your room, Maisie," she murmured, thinking it out. "Goodness knows how we'll fit another bed in there, but Miss Barnes next door would let us have that old canvas cot she keeps in the attic, perhaps. That wouldn't take up much room."

Alice stared at Maisie and her gran with widening eyes. "You'd really let me?" she asked shyly. "Do you mean it?"

Maisie nodded back – she felt shy, too, all of a sudden. "It wouldn't be like your lovely bedroom," she said quietly. "Gran's right, we'll hardly have room to move. And you might miss your parents. Oh! We haven't even thought! What will they say? Will they let you stay without them?"

Alice nodded. "I think so. Mama really was worried about the heat making me ill. And Papa is concerned that something unsavoury is going on.

He would be glad to leave me behind in London, if he knew that I would be looked after. He likes you, Maisie – and I'm sure he would see that you would be a very good person for me to stay with, Mrs Hitchins," she added. She stood up, looking a great deal better. "I shall go home at once and ask."

Alice's father and stepmother sailed for China two days later. Maisie and Alice and Gran went to see them off at Alice's house, the two girls waving their handkerchiefs as the carriage jingled away. Alice had cried a little as her parents climbed into the carriage, but only a tiny bit, and then she wiped her eyes determinedly and hugged Maisie tight.

"I do hope they find out who sank those ships," Maisie murmured, as the carriage disappeared at the end of the road.

Alice's father's mystery did sound so very like the notes in her father's book, which was hidden under her bed in its beautiful Chinese wooden box. It could even be part of the same mystery... Maisie gave a tiny sigh. She could see why Alice hadn't wanted to go to China, but it would be so exciting to travel all that way...

"I wish we could help," Alice whispered, as they hurried back to Albion Street after Gran. "Don't you think we could, Maisie? Somehow?"

"Maybe." Maisie nodded. "Maybe..."

Chapter Three

"What're you two doing, then?"

The growly voice made Maisie and Alice jump. They'd been sitting on the stairs from the hallway, talking with their heads close together, and they hadn't noticed Mr Smith coming down the stairs behind them.

Snowflake, Alice's white cat, sat up and glared at him haughtily, and her two kittens,

Blanche and Lulu, peered out from behind the table legs in the hall. Maisie had left Eddie down in the kitchen with his favourite bone. He was still very miffed about sharing the house with the cats, especially since Snowflake had scratched his nose when he'd sniffed at her. But Alice could hardly have left them all behind. Maisie was hoping that they would get used to each other soon, but at the moment both Eddie and the cats seemed to be sulking.

Maisie jumped up. "Sorry, Mr Smith. We were just chatting." She smiled at him. "If Gran sees me downstairs sitting still, she gives me jobs to do. I just wanted to talk to Alice."

"And Mrs Hitchins doesn't like me helping," Alice put in. "She says I shouldn't, because I'm a young lady, and also because my papa is paying for my board and lodging. But I *like* helping. I do the dusting

46

for Maisie when her gran isn't looking."

"You're good girls." Mr Smith nodded.
"You sit back down, Maisie. I ain't got nothing
needs doing this minute. What were you
two so worried about that you didn't hear
me thumping down the stairs?" He sat down
himself, a few steps further up, sticking his
short legs straight out with a sigh
– he had rheumatism, it
was one of the reasons
he'd given up his
life at sea.

Maisie and Alice exchanged glances. Mr Smith knew about the sea, and ships. Maisie had told Alice about her father's notes – having sworn her to secrecy first – and they were both determined that they had to find out more. But they just weren't sure how to go about it. Perhaps Mr Smith would be able to help?

Alice nodded at Maisie, and Maisie began to explain. "It's Alice's father. We're worried about him, you see. We were thinking about investigating the case here in London, too."

Mr Smith frowned and turned to Alice. "But your father did that, didn't he? He didn't just go haring off to China without trying to find out what was happening here first. How do you two think you're going to discover anything he didn't?"

Maisie shrugged. "Well, everyone at the

shipping office would know Alice's father, wouldn't they?" she pointed out. "He couldn't really ask questions like a detective. No one would tell him anything, in case they got into trouble."

Mr Smith eyed her thoughtfully. "S'pose you've got something there," he admitted. "So what're you planning to do, then?"

Maisie sighed. "That's what we were trying to work out," she admitted. "We don't know where to start. Alice knows more about the shipping business than I do."

"But I don't know very much." Alice shook her head. "We were thinking we could go and look round my father's warehouse at the docks."

Mr Smith sniffed. "Not much of a place for young ladies, down there," he muttered disapprovingly.

Maisie tried not to roll her eyes. Mr Smith was only being kind, but sometimes she wished that people would understand – she was a detective first and a young lady second.

"What if the ships didn't really go down," she asked Mr Smith. "What if it was all a big trick, so someone could sell off the cargoes and the ships, too? Or just repaint them and call them something else. Then the person who really owned the ship – Alice's father – would lose out, but the thief would have a whole new ship, wouldn't they?"

Mr Smith growled. "That's an old, old trick. But I can't say I didn't think of it, Miss Alice, when you were telling your story the other day. It could be, could be… Dangerous, though. We old sailors, we know a ship we've sailed on. A paint job wouldn't fool us."

Maisie nodded. That's exactly what had happened – her father had recognized his old ship.

"And you'd need a crooked crew, to carry off a swindle like that," Mr Smith added. "Though I suppose that ain't so hard to find. And somewhere to get rid of the cargo, afterwards…"

"Do you think any of the ships would come here?" Maisie asked. "The London docks are huge, aren't they? Wouldn't they be a good place to offload the stolen cargoes?"

Mr Smith gave a little snort of laughter. "You're right there. Proper old rabbit warrens, those docks are. Who knows what disappears in and out of there."

He stared at the girls, frowning a little. "Just you be careful, you hear? Don't go sniffing around too deep. Watch yourselves…"

"Maisie! Maisie!"

For once, Maisie was glad to hear Gran calling for her, even though she knew it probably meant more chores. She didn't like the look on Mr Smith's face. It was as though he was about to tell them they shouldn't be heading down to the docks at all.

Of course, they'd still have to go, even if he did warn them off. But perhaps they had better take precautions, Maisie thought, and then she grinned to herself. She knew just the thing…

"You want me to disguise both of you?" Miss Lane's eyes brightened. "Oh yes. Oh, it's such an age since I've dressed you up as a boy,

Maisie. What fun!"

Miss Lane was the actress who lodged
in the rooms on the top floor of 31 Albion
Street. She wasn't home all that often, as she
was busy performing in a new musical revue.
But as it was the middle of the morning the
girls had managed to catch her not only in
but awake. Miss Lane had a huge stock of
clothes that she had worn for various parts,
and stage make-up, too. She had dressed
Maisie to look like a boy before, when Maisie
had been trying to solve the mystery of the
missing money at the local butcher's, where
George worked.

Miss Lane pushed Alice into the middle
of the room and strolled around her
thoughtfully. "Tricky," she said at last.
"Definitely tricky. You're so fair, dear. Not
boyish at all."

"She never goes out in the sun, that's why," Maisie sighed. "Or not without a parasol, anyway."

Alice smiled at her. "It's very boring, you know, always having to wear a hat and gloves, and never getting your nice white boots grubby. Wearing scruffy boys' clothes sounds blissful."

Miss Lane twirled a lock of Alice's silvery-fair hair around her finger. "I suppose we can hide this under a cap. And darken up your cheeks with greasepaint." She smudged some brownish colour expertly over Alice's skin, then she frowned at the rich child's pretty hands, the skin white and soft. "You'll simply have to take her out into the yard and make her scrabble around in some mud," she told Maisie. "No one will ever believe she's a ragamuffin boy with hands like that."

Maisie nodded, and Miss Lane flitted about her rooms, finding caps and jackets and mufflers, which she held up against Maisie and Alice, muttering to herself. "Perhaps this one? No, no, not quite right. Here, put this waistcoat on." The two girls stared at each other, fascinated. All traces of the rich little girl that Alice had been disappeared as she pulled on the tattered garments.

"You look quite different," Maisie murmured to Alice. "You'll have to talk to match, you know."

Alice gazed back at her worriedly. "Will I? I don't know how…"

"Try and sound like George," Maisie suggested. "Just a bit … less nice. And growlier."

Alice made a gruff, squawky sort of noise that sounded a bit like "Hello".

Eddie came out from under Miss Lane's bed where he'd been snoozing and glared at her suspiciously. Then he started to bark, walking round and round the girls, and eyeing them both as though he thought they might be burglars.

"Eddie!" Maisie crouched down to rub his ears. "It's us, you silly dog. You've seen me like this before. Stop it! Shh!"

56

Eddie sank down, growling a little. He didn't like Alice's appearance one bit.

"Well, it must be a good disguise if even Eddie couldn't tell it was me," Alice said, peering into the mirror. "I don't think I look like me at all! But I'm really not sure about changing my voice, Maisie. Maybe I'd better just not talk to anyone?"

Maisie nodded. "Maybe. I suppose if you wrap that muffler around your throat, we can say that you've got a cold if anyone asks."

The two girls thanked Miss Lane and headed cautiously down the stairs to the ground floor. Maisie didn't have any more housework to do – with Alice to help she could get her chores done faster than usual. But Gran would be horrified to see them dressed up in boys' clothes, especially Alice.

She was supposed to be looking after Alice
for her father, not letting her go out in a most
improper disguise.

They slipped out of the front door to
avoid having to go through the kitchen, and
Maisie held her breath until they were round
the corner of Albion Street. They were out!
They'd done it! Alice hugged Maisie and did
a little dance step round the pavement.

"Is that you, Maisie?" someone asked
uncertainly.

Maisie spun round. "No," she muttered,
lowering her voice as much as she could.

"Yes, it is," George said, peering at her
red curls, which were tucked up under a cap.
"I thought someone had stolen that dog
of yours at first. What are you doing? And
who's he?"

Alice giggled, and George looked at her

more closely. "Oh! Sorry, Miss Alice."

"Shh!" Alice told him in a stern whisper.

"I'm a boy. My name's, um, Albert."

"Be quiet, George. You'll spoil everything.
We're detecting – go away!" Maisie said crossly.

George sniffed. "Well, don't go dancing about and cuddling each other in the middle of the street, then. And don't bring the dog! Half the butcher's boys in London probably know him, sausage thief that he is."

Maisie sighed. Eddie had only stolen sausages from George once, but he'd never let her forget it. "He's right, Alice. We'd better be more careful. Remember you're a boy. Put your hands in your pockets and try to slouch a bit."

Alice nodded and hunched her shoulders up to her ears, which made George snort with laughter. "Where are you two off to, anyway?"

"The docks," Maisie whispered.

George frowned. "What, on your own?"

"There's two of us. And Eddie," Maisie pointed out.

George eyed them doubtfully, and Maisie gave a tiny sigh. She knew he wanted to say something like, "But you're just girls…" If Alice hadn't been there, he'd have said it straight out, but she was a proper young lady, and he was being polite.

"We'd better be going," she said firmly. She went to take Alice's hand, then remembered that they were grubby boys and grabbed her sleeve instead.

When she glanced back at the corner of the road, George was still staring after them worriedly.

Chapter Four

"Do you know where we're going?" Maisie whispered to Alice, as she looked up at the huge buildings. They had taken an omnibus and then walked down the Commercial Road to the East India Docks, where Alice's father had a warehouse. It had taken a very long time to get there, and Maisie felt oddly nervous. Usually she loved strange places and new people, but the docks felt like another world, somehow separated from the rest of London. Another city almost. They were so large that she and Alice had been able to see the ships and buildings as they came down the road towards the huge arched entrance. The great masts loomed over the walls and warehouses, dark against the grey sky.

"Oh yes." Alice nodded confidently. "Papa brought me here several times. Don't worry, Maisie. I know my way around."

But Maisie couldn't help feeling anxious. She hadn't expected the docks to have such high walls – they wouldn't be able to sneak in unnoticed, as she'd planned. Instead, they'd have to march through the archway and look as though they were meant to be there.

"No one will suspect us, Maisie," Alice promised. "Most of the men here come every morning to ask for work. They'll be taken on if there's a ship to be unloaded, and if there isn't, they won't make any money that day. It's a hard life. But it means that we can be two boys hoping to earn pennies running errands or carrying boxes."

"I suppose so," Maisie murmured, trying to march along confidently as they passed through the archway. She needn't have worried, as no one seemed to be taking the slightest bit of notice.

In front of them sprawled the great enclosed import dock, surrounded by wharves – long platforms for the ships to moor up against. Alice had tried to explain all the different words to Maisie, but it was confusing. At least the dock basin was what it sounded like, though. As far as Maisie could tell, it was just a big bowl of water. The ships waited there to go through the locks and on into the docks themselves. The locks were like gates that shut the docks off from the river, so that the ships moored in them stayed level even when the river went up and down with the tides. Otherwise, Alice had pointed out, the ships would be moving up and down while they were being unloaded.

The ships moored in the import dock towered over the two girls, making Maisie feel small and out of place. Everyone they passed was in a hurry, trundling along with barrels and boxes and trolleys. What made it even stranger was that her father would probably know exactly where he was going, Maisie thought, rather sadly. He would probably have brought a ship in here some time. Even if he hadn't, he would still understand this world more than Maisie ever could.

"Out of the way!" someone roared, and Maisie froze, not sure where to move. There were so many people rushing around – was someone shouting at them?

Alice skipped aside as a porter came huffing past with a heavily loaded trolley.

She dragged Maisie after her, giggling. She didn't seem to be bothered at all – it was as if she hardly noticed the hulking ships.

"If we go down here, we'll get to the warehouse where the goods from Papa's ships are stored," Alice explained.

"They're huge," Maisie murmured, looking around. "Do all these warehouses belong to merchants like your papa, then?"

Alice glanced at her in surprise. "No, he doesn't own the warehouse, it belongs to the dock company. Several merchants rent warehouse space here, like Papa does. Just space to store the cargoes. His main establishment is in the city." She sighed. "But that building is quite expensive to rent. Papa may have to give it up."

"You know a lot about his business," Maisie told her, feeling a little envious. She knew so little about her own father's life at sea – just those strange notes he had sent her.

Alice wrinkled her nose. "Only bits. Papa likes to talk to me, and I love to hear him explain about the cargoes the ships are carrying and where they have come from.

People have been drinking tea in China for thousands of years, did you know that? Long before anyone ever drank it here." She shivered. "I do hope Papa and Mama are well. Mama gets a little seasick. She told me before she left that she hoped she would get used to the motion of the waves after a day or so. But she will be so worn out by the time they reach China. It will take weeks and weeks to get there, even though they're going on a fast steamship."

Maisie nodded. The ship her father worked on had no steam engine, only sails. He had told her in his letters that he was leaving the sea because steamships were slowly but surely taking over the East India business that he'd known most of his life. There wasn't much place for a sailing ship in the tea trade now, when the steamers could cut through the Suez Canal to the Mediterranean, instead of going all the way around the coast of Africa. That way they knocked weeks off the journey. Sailing ships couldn't go through the canal, her father had told her, because the winds blew the wrong way. It seemed strange that something as subtle and changeable as the direction of the wind could be so important.

"Who are those men over there?" Maisie whispered to Alice. "The smartly dressed ones."

The two men looked very different from the porters in their ragged jackets and neckerchiefs. They had smart suits on, with waistcoats, and one of them had a gold watch chain stretched across his plump front.

"Clerks," Alice murmured, as they sidled

closer and lurked behind a pile of cloth-wrapped bales. Eddie sniffed at them, and then slumped down for a snooze. It had been a long walk for a small dog. "They must work for the dock company, or perhaps one of the merchants. There's a lot of counting and lists to make, you see, when the ships are being unloaded."

The two men seemed to be talking about a music-hall show that they had been to the previous night – they were arguing about the conjuror. "I tell you, he made it disappear!" the younger man protested, as he ran a comb over his slicked black hair. It was shining with hair oil, and it made Maisie shudder.

"That rabbit did *not* disappear, Bertie. There was a trapdoor, or some such." The other clerk rolled his eyes. Then he elbowed

Bertie in the ribs. "Next you'll be claiming that old Lacey's ships *disappeared*. Was that magic, then?"

Maisie and Alice stared at each other, and leaned closer.

"Who knows?" Bertie shook his head. "He's gone off to China to investigate, did you hear that?"

The other clerk looked surprised. "Really? So it isn't some sort of swindle, then? Lacey didn't sink them himself?"

Maisie grabbed Alice's arm. Her friend's cheeks had flushed suddenly scarlet, and it looked as though she was about to dash out of their hiding place and tell the two clerks that it wasn't true and her father was an honest man.

"Shh!" Maisie hissed, slapping her hand across Alice's mouth.

"What was that?" Bertie asked, starting towards the bales. "Someone skulking back there?"

Alice gave Maisie a horrified glance and the two girls looked around them anxiously. They were tucked tightly behind the bales, and there was no way to get out without the men seeing them and knowing that they'd been spying. They would be kicked out of the dockyard – or worse.

"We'll just have to brazen it out," Maisie muttered. "Let me do the talking," she added in a gruff whisper, trying to find her boy's voice.

But Eddie had sensed their panic. He jumped up and peered round the bales, wondering why the girls sounded so scared. When he saw two perfectly friendly looking gentlemen, he trotted out, his tail wagging.

"A dog! Scruffy little beast."

"Must have been ratting. Good boy, aren't you?"

Maisie peeped out and saw Bertie scratching Eddie behind the ears, while Eddie drooled at him delightedly, and then rolled over on to his back.

"Half the rats in the warehouse are bigger than he is," the other man snorted. "Still, I suppose the little beggar can get down the holes after the brutes. Come on, Bertie, better get back to work, I suppose."

The two men sauntered away, and Eddie pattered back to Maisie and Alice, looking smug.

"Oh, you're such a good boy!" Maisie hugged him.

"I'm sorry, Maisie," Alice whispered, crouching down to pat Eddie's nose. "I'm not very good at this spying thing. I got so angry when he said that about Papa!"

Maisie put an arm round her friend's shoulders. "Perhaps it was good, though. Now you know to keep quiet."

"Oh, I do!" Alice agreed. "What shall we do next? We could try and see where they went? Maybe they'll say something else about the case? I promise to be perfectly silent," she added hurriedly.

"Maybe." Maisie chewed her bottom lip. For such a busy place, there seemed to be surprisingly little gossiping going on. The unloading was so noisy, the dockworkers probably couldn't hear well enough to chat. They'd been lucky to catch those two clerks. "Or we could look at the cargo from your father's ships. Perhaps that would give us a clue?"

"Oh yes." Alice nodded, and they sneaked out from behind the bales, threading their way carefully along the quay. Alice peered into the cavernous warehouses as they passed, checking the numbers painted over the doors and looking for the right one. "Here," she murmured at last. "This is the one. It's almost empty." She swallowed sadly. "The cargoes were all lost."

Maisie looked round the little door that was cut into the great front doors of the warehouse. The main ones would be opened when there was a ship moored at the wharf in front to unload. Today the warehouse looked dark and empty, with just a few shafts of sunlight cutting through the dusty air. Some boxes were piled up at the back, but that was all.

"Let's go and look at those," she whispered to Alice. "No one's here."

The girls crept into the warehouse and stood staring down at the boxes. Several of them were open, the nails pulled out of the wooden lids, and Maisie was just about to lift one of them off, when heavy footsteps shook the boarded floor.

"Just what do you two brats think you're up to?"

Maisie let out a squeak, and then immediately coughed, trying to sound growly and boyish. "Nothing," she croaked. But she could hear how suspicious she sounded – she might as well have just admitted that they were snooping around, looking for clues.

The huge man towering over them gave a whistly sort of laugh and rubbed his hands together. Maisie shivered and felt Alice huddle close up against her. He looked like

he was going to throw them into the dirty

water of the dock. And enjoy it…

Eddie let out a breathy little snarl, and Maisie scooped him up. If he tried to bite, the docker would probably wring his neck. Eddie growled and wriggled, as if he was eager to hunt, and Maisie remembered the two clerks. "We're just ratting," she burst out. "Mr Jones said to." *Surely there's a Mr Jones at the docks somewhere*, she thought. "One ran in between these boxes, a great big one. With yellow teeth."

The man stared at the pile of boxes and took a step back. He looked Maisie and Alice up and down, scowling. "Something funny about you two," he muttered. "Just can't put my finger on it. Get on out of here. And if I see you hanging around again, I'll stick you in a barrel, like that poor feller we found on the *Golden Lady*." He snorted with laughter at their horrified faces. "Didn't hear about

that one, then? All nailed up in a barrel.
She came over from China – we unloaded
her Tuesday last. And the smell! Half the
quayside lost their breakfasts into the
water… Now, go on, hop it, before I change
my mind!"

Chapter Five

They hardly spoke on the way back to Albion Street. Maisie was worried about Alice – she was so white and frightened-looking. She wasn't used to people shouting at her, ever. As they ducked into the yard behind the house, Maisie caught her arm.

"Please say something," she begged, staring at Alice. "I know it was scary. I'm sorry, I shouldn't have taken you there... We shouldn't have gone. It was too dangerous."

Alice's eyes widened. "Maisie, we went to the docks because I want to help Papa! And you want to find out about your father's mystery, too. You didn't *make* me go! That man was frightening... But he was mostly talking to you, not me." She smiled, a slightly trembly little smile. "Which meant he wasn't looking when I found this." She took off her big peaked cap and pulled out a delicate little china plate, painted with golden flowers.

"You had that plate *on your head* all the way home?" Maisie gasped. "You took that from the warehouse? What if he'd caught you?"

"I had to!" Alice hissed. "I didn't just do it for fun, Maisie, look at it!"

Maisie took the plate, stroking the thin, translucent china. "It's beautiful," she agreed. "But I still don't see— Oh!" She looked at the pattern again, frowning. "It's the same as the one on that pretty set in your drawing room."

"Exactly," Alice said triumphantly. "The boxes hidden at the back were full of it."

"So?" Maisie shook her head. "I don't understand. There's more china like it in the warehouse, so what?"

"That set in our drawing room was a sample that Papa's agent in China sent.

To see if he liked it and to ask if he should send more over. There was only that one set in the whole country, Maisie! Papa said yes, but that cargo of precious china is what went down with the *Sarah-Rose*!" Alice folded her arms. "Or that's what Papa was told."

"So that plate is proof that the *Sarah-Rose* didn't sink?" Maisie gasped.

Alice nodded. "No wonder they didn't want anyone snooping around."

Maisie and Alice were sitting on Maisie's bed, leaning against the wall. It was only late afternoon, but they were both exhausted from the long journey to the docks and from their terrifying encounter with the man in the warehouse. Maisie had her father's notebook open on her lap, but she wasn't really reading it, just flicking idly through the pages.

Alice smothered a ladylike yawn. "We know that Papa was right – those ships didn't just sink, or at least the *Sarah-Rose* didn't. But what do we do about it?"

"I suppose someone at the docks must have put those boxes there," Maisie said thoughtfully. "Maybe that horrible man who chased us away. He *looked* suspicious. If only we could find out for sure."

Alice shuddered and huddled closer to Maisie. "We'll have to go back, won't we?"

Maisie nodded. "Perhaps to the clerks' rooms, if we could get in there. They might know more about the different cargoes. But maybe we should go as ourselves this time and explain why we're there, don't you think?" Alice didn't answer, and Maisie looked down at her anxiously, but then she smiled. Alice was asleep against her shoulder. Maisie flicked over another couple of pages, tracing her fingers over one of her father's little drawings, and then gradually her head slipped forward and she slept, too.

"Maisie!"

Alice sounded horrified and Maisie woke up with a jump. She had been dreaming about that man in the warehouse, except that in her dream he was even bigger, and there was a whole stack of barrels lined up behind him, and he had been about to squash her and Alice into one of them… Maisie shook her head firmly. It was only a dream.

"What is it?" she asked sleepily. "Is my gran calling us?"

"No, look!" Alice shook her arm. "Maisie, look what Eddie's done!"

Maisie peered down at the little dog, who was lying on the bed next to her. Had he been chasing Snowflake, or the kittens? He hadn't *hurt* them, had he? Maisie looked around worriedly for telltale wisps of white fur. But amazingly enough, Snowflake was curled up on her bed, too, on the other side of Alice, and the kittens were chasing a feather under Alice's little folding cot.

She looked back at Eddie and for a moment thought he was chewing on one of his bones. Then she realized why Alice sounded so shocked. He was nibbling at her father's notebook. The spine was almost completely chewed away.

"Oh, Eddie, no!" Maisie wailed, snatching it from him. Pages sagged out of the book, and the front cover fell off. "Oh no, oh no," she murmured, scrabbling for the pages, and Eddie peered up at her in surprise. Then his ears drooped guiltily. He didn't understand what he had done wrong, but he could tell that Maisie wasn't happy.

"Maybe it tasted salty, because of the sea," Maisie sighed. "Oh, Eddie. All my father's notes! And he asked me to look after them." Her voice wobbled.

Snowflake padded on to Alice's lap and flicked her whiskers smugly at Eddie. But he didn't even growl. He crawled off the bed and went to hide himself underneath it.

"Maisie, what's that?" Alice asked suddenly, picking up the back cover of the notebook as it slithered away from the binding completely and flumped on to the bed. "Look, that's not how it's supposed to be, is it?"

"There's something in there," Maisie murmured, sitting up a little straighter and taking the limp, chewed thing from Alice. The cover wasn't just one piece of card, as she'd thought. It had been folded over, to make a sort of pocket. And inside the pocket were a handful of small pieces of paper that cascaded out as she tipped it up. They were covered in tiny handwriting. Her father's handwriting.

"Secret notes…" Maisie whispered. She fanned them out across the bed, frowning down at them. "My father didn't want anybody to see these – not even me."

"Maybe we shouldn't read them…" Alice suggested doubtfully, but Maisie shook her head.

"We have to. What if there's something important? Something that might let us help your father?" She didn't tell Alice what she had seen as the papers scattered down on to the patchwork quilt. The name Lacey, underlined as though it was significant with a great dark scratch of pencil.

"There are dates, so we can put them in order," she murmured, starting to sort out the little pieces. "Here's the first, look."

November 8th

Can't write this in my commonplace book any longer. Too many prying eyes around here. Too dangerous. Only just starting to be able to think clearly and write again. Bedridden for almost a week. The crew say that it was a block come loose from the rigging, it swung down and hit me over the back of the head. But I have my doubts. If it was a block, it was loosened from its rope on purpose. Someone wants me kept quiet. Pity for them that I have such a hard head!

But I will have to play the fool for

a while now, and not let them see that I suspect. Ha! I don't even know who it is I'm suspecting!

November 15th

Gossip going around the port here is that Mr <u>Lacey</u> is going to get himself into trouble. He won't leave well alone and say goodbye to his sunken ships as he should. Poor man. He must suspect, as I do, that those ships of his are safe and sound. Each of them is tucked away in another harbour under another name.

January 6th

So angry. I blame myself. I should never have mentioned my thoughts to the captain, but I knew that he was honest

- somehow I could tell. I warned him not to go digging about! He should have listened! Lost overboard? Never. Captain Morris had the best sea legs of any man, he would never have slipped and fallen over the rail. It's nonsense - the poor captain was asking too many questions. Very glad that I have hidden these notes. Have made sure to make a sad entry into the main part of the book, grieving for the captain and his dreadful "accident"! Am sure that someone is reading everything I write.

"He did!" Maisie gasped. "He wrote it in the notebook, I remember reading it again before I went to sleep a couple of nights ago. He said that due to a terrible misfortune,

the dear captain had been swept overboard,
perhaps by a freak wave."

"I read it, too…" Alice whispered shakily.
"Oh, Maisie, this is dreadful! These men
killed your father's captain! They already
suspect your father, and now *my* father
is going to China to stir them up all over
again!"

Maisie gulped. "I know." She put her hand
in Alice's, squeezing her friend's cold fingers.
"So we shall simply have to solve the mystery
before your father's ship arrives."

Maisie peered at the little squares of paper
again. Her candle was guttering and almost
burnt down – it wouldn't last much longer.
But she couldn't go to sleep yet. She had been
reading and rereading the notes ever since

she and Alice had gone to bed, desperate to find another clue. They had been so worried and silent at supper that Gran had started talking about Mrs Winslow's Soothing Syrup, or cod liver oil. Maisie had eaten a whole extra helping of boiled turnip, just to prove how very healthy she was. She could still taste it.

Eddie sighed and wriggled in his sleep, and the little paper squares fluttered. Maisie patted him gently – she had forgiven him for chewing the book now, of course. Then she pulled out one of the notes that had ended up squashed under his front paw. She turned it over to smooth it out properly – and gasped, holding her candle closer.

There was more writing on the other side of the note.

December 25th

Overheard two sailors in a harbour drinking den tonight. Talking of the disappearing ships. Nothing new to say, except "the ivy". They said "the ivy got them". What does that mean? Ivy doesn't grow at sea! Some sort of clinging water weed? Stupid... Besides, I'm sure they mentioned something about London, too. I just couldn't hear it properly. Ivy... Who knows. Unless it's a person, perhaps. Mr Ivy, or Ivey. Aivy, maybe - of course I've not seen it written. Probably nothing, but it niggles at me. Ivy...

Maisie sighed to herself. She had no idea what it meant either. And she was never going to get to sleep now. The mystery was so exciting, and at the same time so hard to get hold of. It ran through her fingers like water.

She wriggled out of bed, leaving Eddie snoring a little, and crept round Alice and the three cats on the folding cot. She padded slowly into the kitchen to make herself a cup of cocoa. Maisie was halfway to the stove before she realized that she wasn't the only person in the room. Mr Smith was sitting at the kitchen table, frowning. Spread in front of him was a piece of paper with writing on, but as he saw Maisie looking, he quickly folded it up and stowed it in his pocket.

Maisie smiled at him, wondering why the message was so secret. A love note, perhaps! She liked the idea of Mr Smith sighing over some lady. It would be nice for him to have company, as Maisie worried that he was rather lonely.

The note had been hand-delivered, she had seen that as he'd folded it away. *Noah Smith*, it said in large black letters on the back. Someone had slipped it through the door for Mr Smith to find. And perhaps he had been down here ever since, worrying over it. Not a love letter, then… The writing looked faintly familiar, Maisie thought, stifling a yawn. Perhaps she had seen it on another of Mr Smith's letters?

"I can't sleep, Mr Smith." Maisie smiled at him brightly. "Would you fancy a cup of cocoa with me?"

The old ship's cook heaved a mighty sigh and said, "Aye, Maisie. Aye, I would." His glass eye seemed to be fixed on her, glinting in the light of the lamp. "You're a good girl, Maisie. Your father would be so proud of you."

Maisie was poking at the ashes in the stove, trying to get the fire going again to heat the milk, but she turned round at the mention of her father. "Mr Smith, did you say you lost your eye on board your ship? It was an accident, wasn't it? Was it because of a falling block? My father said in his last letter that someone on the ship was hit by one falling from the rigging. What did he mean?"

Mr Smith nodded wisely. "Common injury on board ships, Maisie. A block – hmmm. Hard to explain. A great big lump of wood with holes in it, that's what you'd think if you saw one, I suppose. The ropes run through it – it's part of a pulley, you see, to make it easier to haul the sails up and down. But if the end of the rope is loose, the block can run down the rope and hit someone walking below."

"Oh." Maisie nodded thoughtfully. "And you got hit by one?"

"No, no. It was a flying rope end that did for me. Thrashing about in a gale. Took my eye straight out."

Maisie shuddered. Life at sea could obviously be dangerous and her father's injury could have been an accident. But somehow she didn't think it very likely.

Chapter Six

Maisie found it very hard to drag herself
out of bed the next morning. She'd had so
little sleep that her mind felt foggy and dull.
Alice was talking to her as they buttoned up
each other's dresses, but her friend's voice
sounded strangely like the twittering of little
birds.

"Maisie, are you listening? Oh, Maisie,

you're still half asleep!" Alice patted her cheek gently. "Are you all right?"

"I couldn't get to sleep until late," Maisie explained, yawning. "I kept reading those notes, over and over. But it's a good thing I did – look." She handed Alice the note with the writing on the back.

"A clue!" Alice breathed. "What can it mean? Ivy?" She frowned. "There was a tree in our garden that had to be cut down, because ivy grew all around it. Papa said that it had sucked the life out of the tree. The ivy strangled it." Her face went suddenly white. "Do you think this Mr Ivy is a strangler, Maisie?"

Maisie shuddered. "I hope not. And we don't even know that Ivy is a person! That was just an idea my father came up with. But even if he is a person, and he is a strangler

– ugh – we shall have to go on, Alice. We can't let your father and stepmother sail into danger like this. And if my father is right and this Ivy is in London, then we are the only ones in the right place to stop it."

Alice nodded, but she was still pale. "I was telling you before, Maisie, I think we should go to Papa's office in the city. It's in Threadneedle Street. I'm wondering if there are any papers there that we can look at for more clues. Perhaps Papa even knows this Mr Ivy, but has no reason to suspect him?" She looked uncertainly at Maisie. "I know it seems a bit far-fetched, but I can't think what else to do..."

"Not nearly as far-fetched as some of the plans I was thinking up in the middle of the night. Oh, excuse me!" Maisie stifled a mammoth yawn, and then giggled. "I think we should go as soon as I've helped Gran with the washing up and done the dusting. If we leave it any later, I'll just fall asleep."

But it was as if Gran had heard them planning and was trying to prevent them setting off to do what she described as "that unladylike detecting". Every time Maisie finished a chore, Gran would pop up with another and she kept shooing Alice away whenever she tried to help. Gran kept telling her that a nice young lady like Alice should sit with her embroidery in the lodgers' sitting room – which was a gloomy room full of wax flowers that hardly anyone ever used. Alice kept sneaking out to give Maisie a hand when Gran wasn't looking, but it was still halfway through the afternoon by the time the two girls finally made their way to the front door.

"Come on, Alice," Maisie gasped, flinging

on her mantle and shivering in the chill

February mist. "Oh, I thought she was never

going to stop."

"I know! The house must be spotless now.

Shall we take a horse bus down along Oxford Street?" Alice asked hopefully. She had never travelled on the omnibuses before coming to live with Maisie, and she liked watching the other passengers.

Maisie nodded. "Do you know the people at your father's office? What are we going to say to them?"

Alice nodded. "I've been trying to think," she said, peering along the road to look for an omnibus approaching. "Oh, it's coming, Maisie. Can we sit on the top?"

Maisie sighed. She thought it was far too cold to sit on the open top of the carriage, but at least it would stop her falling asleep.

They settled on the long bench on the top deck, with Eddie held tightly on Maisie's lap. She was glad of him – he was like a little furry hot water bottle.

Once Alice had taken a few minutes to
admire the shops, she turned back to Maisie.
"I have a plan," she said, rather mysteriously.
"For Papa's office. I'm going to tell the clerks
that I want to find my necklace. Papa took it
to work with him a few weeks ago because
the clasp was broken. He was going to take
it to a jeweller's for me. But of course with

everything that was happening he didn't have time."

"And you're going to say that you'll take it to be mended yourself?" Maisie nodded admiringly.

"Yes, because hopefully Papa will have put it in a drawer somewhere, and we shall have to look all over his private office for it." Alice looked pleased with herself. "It's rather a good excuse, isn't it? We just have to hope that it isn't just lying there on the top of his desk."

They rattled on through the streets into the City, where Alice had explained that there were a great many shipping merchants and bankers and lawyers. "Everything to do with money," she had said vaguely.

Eventually, they wobbled down the outside staircase of the bus as it pulled up in Threadneedle Street. Maisie stared at the grand columns on the front of the huge Bank of England. Alice had been there often enough not to be impressed, and she hauled Maisie past impatiently.

"This is a very smart sort of place to have an office," Maisie murmured, removing her mantle.

"I know," Alice sighed. "Papa doesn't want to give the rooms up, because then everyone will know that the business is in trouble. But he might have to soon. We're here, look." She pointed to a brass plate engraved with *Lacey and Co.* fixed up beside a huge black door. Then she led Maisie up the steps and into a grand hallway with a gilded lift and a boy in a smart uniform to work it.

"Second floor, please," Alice told him, and Maisie tried not to giggle as the lift lurched upwards and her stomach lurched with it.

"Good afternoon, Miss Eccles," Alice said politely to the smartly dressed lady clerk in the outer office.

"Oh! Miss Lacey. How very nice to see you."

Maisie wasn't sure that she meant it. Miss Eccles looked very slightly worried and she fiddled with the papers on her desk. Perhaps she thought that Alice had come to check up on her. After all, her employer had sailed away to China, so she might not have been working very hard.

"I've come to find my necklace – did Papa mention it to you, Miss Eccles?" Alice asked. She was trying very hard to be believable, Maisie realized. Alice wasn't very good at acting a part (or lying, as Gran would have called it). If Miss Eccles had known her well, she would have noticed that Alice's cheeks had gone bright pink, and she was playing with her hair.

"A necklace?"

"Yes, Papa was supposed to take it to be mended, but I think he must have forgotten. Or perhaps he just didn't have time before he went away. Do you know where he put it?"

Alice smiled hopefully at the clerk, but she
had her fingers crossed behind her back – of
course they were hoping that Miss Eccles
didn't know.

"No, I'm afraid he never mentioned it." Miss Eccles shook her head.

"Oh, how very annoying." Alice was trying hard not to sound too relieved. "Well, never mind, we shall just have to go and look for it." She started to walk towards the door of her father's private office.

"But you can't go in there!" Miss Eccles yelped.

Alice blinked at her, and Maisie looked at the clerk curiously. Why didn't she want them to go in?

"Why ever not?" Alice asked, and her cold voice wasn't put on this time.

"Mr Lacey is very particular about his office," Miss Eccles explained. "He specifically asked that no one should use the office while he was away. Even I don't go in there unless he calls me!"

"That certainly doesn't apply to me!" Alice snapped. And she marched straight over to open the door. Maisie followed her, and Eddie whisked in after them.

Alice shut the door with a decided thud, and the two girls leaned against it, staring at each other.

"I can't tell whether she was trying to keep us out or if she's just fussy," Maisie gasped. "You were amazing! So brave!"

"I just copied the voice Papa uses when he thinks people are being rude. He's much better at it than I am – he can freeze your blood." Alice giggled. "But she did look quite shocked. We'd better hurry and look around before she finds an excuse to get rid of us."

Maisie nodded. "This office is awfully tidy, Alice. I suppose most of the records are kept in those cabinets outside." There were no papers lying on the big desk, and when they tried the drawers, there was very little in them apart from headed writing paper, blotters and a fountain pen. And Alice's necklace, in a little velvet box. She tucked it away inside her fur muff.

"Nothing useful at all," Alice sighed.

"There is one thing, though," Maisie said thoughtfully, as she closed the last of the drawers and went to look at the bookshelf. "Miss Eccles was lying. She does come in here, and often enough to leave a trace of her scent. Can't you smell it?"

Alice sniffed. "Lavender? I thought that was the furniture polish."

"No, she was wearing lavender scent. I noticed because it's quite old-fashioned, and her dress is so very new and smart. It was a beautiful dark silk, did you see?"

"No, you know you're much better at noticing that sort of thing, Maisie." Alice shook her head crossly. "I suppose she comes in here to sit on the comfortable armchair and eat her lunch, or something like that. Oh, I don't think there's anything useful here

117

at all. I was sure we would find some clue about Ivy! It just isn't fair!"

"Perhaps we could try asking Miss Eccles? If she's not too cross to talk to us." Maisie went quietly over to the door and pulled it open, revealing Miss Eccles standing just on the other side, looking rather surprised.

"Did you want something?" Maisie asked her sweetly.

"I was just coming to see if you had found the necklace," the clerk said, sounding huffy.

"Yes, thank you." Alice brought out the box, opening it up to show a beautiful amethyst necklace.

"Very pretty." Miss Eccles's hand went to her wrist, Maisie noticed, to stroke a gold charm bracelet she was wearing, as though Alice's necklace had reminded her of it.

"That's nice," Maisie said politely, wanting

to butter Miss Eccles up so they could ask her some questions. "They're lovely charms. So delicate!"

"Oh!" Miss Eccles smiled. "They are, aren't they? They all have a meaning. I was born in Yorkshire, so this is a white rose, and this little pony is to remind me of the pony I had as a girl."

Maisie nodded – and then her eyes widened. Her voice was a little hoarse as she said, "I think the ivy leaf is the prettiest. Such a nice green colour. Why … why do you have that one?"

Miss Eccles smiled. "Oh, that was the first one that I was given, when I was a very small girl. My name is Ivy, you see."

Chapter Seven

Maisie wasn't quite sure how they got themselves out of the Lacey and Co. offices. It seemed that they were suddenly just outside on the street, staring blankly at each other. At last, Maisie grabbed Alice by the arm and hurried her along the road to a church with a little courtyard, and they sat down upon the wall. Alice's face shone sickly white, even in the late-afternoon shadows.

"It's her!" Alice gasped. "It's her! Papa's clerk! She has worked for him for years, he told me. He trusted her. She knew almost more about the business than he did, he said. Her father was a merchant, but he fell on hard times and lost his business, so Miss Eccles went out to work. It was terribly sad."

"Could that be why she's doing all this?" Maisie asked doubtfully. "If her father was ruined?"

"You mean, it's all revenge?" Alice's eyes widened even more.

"I don't know! Maybe she just really hated being poor. Perhaps she's trying to make as much money as she possibly can?"

"You two all right? You look white as a sheet, Maisie. Your freckles are almost dark brown."

"George!" Maisie jumped up in surprise, and Eddie growled suspiciously. He knew quite well that George didn't like him. "Have you been following us?"

"No," George said quickly, but he didn't sound very convincing. Then he shrugged and added, "Maybe. Saw you heading off again. And then that Mr Smith that lodges with you came out the front of the house, all scowling. Said did I know where you was, because he was worried you'd gone off to the docks. I didn't tell him I'd seen you, but I thought I'd keep an eye on you myself. I was on the bottom of that horse bus. And then I just hung around outside. That your pa's offices, Miss Alice?"

"We don't need keeping an eye on," Maisie muttered, but she didn't sound very cross. If Miss Eccles was the evil mastermind behind the sinking of all those ships, and possibly even pushing people overboard and nailing bodies up in barrels then it would be best to have as many people as possible on the case.

"We've found out who it is that arranged for Papa's ships to be sunk," Alice told him impressively. "But I don't know what we can do about it. I'm not sure the police will believe us, Maisie. Not just on the strength of a charm bracelet…"

"A what?" George looked bewildered, and they pulled him down to sit next to them on the wall and explained. Then they explained it again, because George said they weren't making any more sense than his Aunt Lucy, who could only ever tell a story backwards. But eventually he let out a slow, surprised whistle.

"I think you have solved it and all. But you've still got to prove it. And stop her!"

"How though?" Maisie muttered.

"We've got to keep her under observation," George said, drawing out the long word to show off. "Watch her," he added, in case they hadn't understood.

Alice jumped up, pulling at Maisie's arm. "We'd better go, then."

"What?" Maisie looked at her in surprise. "Where?"

"After her. Look – she's just gone past the church! I'm sure it's her, Maisie, I saw that hat with the bird on it hanging on the coat stand in the office." She hurried to the gate, and Maisie and George dashed after her. "Look, there, do you see? She's got a smart dark green coat, with a fur trim."

"That looks ever so expensive," Maisie said, as they ran out into the street. "A silk dress and a fur-trimmed coat. Could she be buying all that on the wages your father pays her?"

Alice shook her head. "Probably not."

"She might have saved up for them,"

George pointed out. "But it does seem like she's richer than she should be," he added quickly, when Maisie and Alice glared at him. "Here, slow down a bit. We don't want to get too close, in case she spots us."

They dropped back a little, but it was already getting dark. They couldn't risk falling too far behind, in case they lost Ivy Eccles's dark coat in among the hurrying people on the pavements.

"I think she's making for the docks," Maisie whispered, after they'd gone a little further on. "Look, we're coming out on to the Commercial Road."

"Did she suspect us?" Alice gasped. "Perhaps she realized we were looking for clues in the office and she's going to hide the evidence."

Maisie frowned. "She can't have suspected. She'd never have told us about the charm then, would she? No, we're just lucky. Now we'll get to see what she's doing. If we can get into the docks without anyone stopping us, that is…"

George snorted. "Useless, you are. We just need to wait for a cart and duck down beside it."

Maisie rolled her eyes. "Very well then, Mr Know-It-All. You can be in charge of that."

George stepped in front, sticking out his chest importantly and, as they came up to the gate, he gestured to them to press up against the wall. They skulked by the archway until a cart came lumbering past, and then George beckoned them hurriedly through. Maisie hadn't thought that such a simple plan would work, but no one shouted after them.

The docks were even stranger by night, Maisie thought, shivering a little. In the half dark the ships loomed over them like monsters in the mist, and the noises seemed louder than they ever had in daylight. The water lapped quietly against the stone walls of the dock, over and over again, like whispering voices. Every so often there was a slapping noise, as the ships' rigging moved in the wind, followed by the creaking of old timbers. She was very glad that she wasn't alone.

"Look, isn't that Miss Eccles? Down there – by your papa's warehouse." Maisie pointed and they tiptoed after her. The figure melted into a pool of shadow, and then the shadow broke apart again, moving out towards a great sailing ship moored at the dock. Now, there were two shadows – Miss Eccles had met an accomplice. There was a tiny hiss as one of them struck a Lucifer match, and then a flare of yellow light that died away to the faintest glow.

"Dark lantern," George muttered. "Got shutters to hide the light, so you can signal with it. And hide your light if you don't want to be seen, more to the point… Still, there's enough light to see the size of him, though. Look. He's huge…"

"It's that man! The one who shouted at us in the warehouse," Alice hissed, moving closer to Maisie.

"It makes sense that he'd be working for her," Maisie whispered back. "We need to get closer, so we can hear what they're saying." But she didn't move. She couldn't help thinking about the way that enormous man had smiled when he told them about the body in the barrel...

"What's that ship got on the front of it?" George murmured, peering through the shadows. "A girl. Looks like she's got a tail."

"Figureheads, they all have figureheads," Alice told him impatiently. "It's just to make them look nice. That's a mermaid."

Maisie blinked. "Is it?" She squinted, but she couldn't see well enough. Forgetting to be frightened, she started to sneak closer. She heard Alice gasp behind her, and then the tiniest padding of footsteps as her two friends followed her towards the ship and the conspirators.

"He's still digging about, Jacob," Miss Eccles was saying, as Maisie ducked into a patch of deep shadow. The three of them were lurking under the metal framework of a crane now. Maisie thought it must be used for unloading the heavy cargo. "He's gone off to China to find out what happened to the ships."

"That Lacey," Jacob growled. "Doesn't he ever give up? We need to get rid of him, Miss Ivy. He's getting to be more trouble than he's worth."

"He trusts me, though," Ivy Eccles murmured. "It's useful to have the run of the office, to be able to read his letters… If he has an *accident*, someone else will buy Lacey and Co. and I'll need to build up that trust all over again. Still. You may be right, we might just have to start again. Lacey's daughter was at the offices this afternoon, nasty spoilt little brat. I'm sure she was nosing about – she said she was looking for a necklace, but I wouldn't trust her as far as I could throw her. She was definitely looking for information, even if she didn't suspect me."

"What about the ship?" Jacob sounded nervous. "If they're suspicious, Miss Ivy… Perhaps the *Elizabeth Ann* had better have an accident, too. They might be able to trace her back here."

"Yes. What a waste." Miss Eccles sighed, and looked up at the figurehead. The huge man turned to look at the mermaid as well, and the pinprick of light from his dark lantern fell upon the wooden face. It was thickly painted, the skin creamy white and the eyes deep blue, with heavy black brows.

But in the lantern light, Maisie could clearly see the tears trailing down the pale cheeks. The resin beads were just as her father had described them.

It was the weeping mermaid.

"There's a cargo of brandy in that warehouse behind," Jacob murmured. "Small kegs, easy to lift. We'll douse her in brandy, and she'll go up like a torch. Don't you worry, Miss Ivy. No one will know."

"We can't let them set fire to the ship!" Maisie whispered. "The evidence! We need to get the police! Come on, let's go."

The three of them started to back away slowly, desperate to turn and run, but knowing that it wasn't safe, that they had to be so, so quiet. As they reached the bow of the boat next to the *Elizabeth Ann*, Maisie drew a deep breath, feeling a little safer. "Let's run," she whispered to the others, and the three of them began to hurry along the side of the quay, with the dark water glinting below.

Maisie looked round to check that Miss Ivy and her henchman weren't following.

No, they were clear away, a good three warehouses behind. But when she turned back, she found that she and Eddie were alone. George and Alice had disappeared. And then a strong, iron-hard arm shot out and grabbed her, too, hauling her into the darkness between two piles of crates.

Chapter Eight

Maisie gasped and kicked and tried to bite the hand that was pressed tightly across her mouth. She heard a scrabble of paws, and then Eddie began to bark frantically, and the person holding her – a man, whose voice was strangely familiar – groaned, "Noah, you didn't tell me the dog was here!"

"Sorry, Dan!"

Maisie wriggled harder. She definitely knew *that* voice.

"If you stop struggling and promise not to shout, I'll let you go," the man holding her muttered. "We're friends. Friends, Maisie, I promise you. We've come to help."

"Help!" growled the other man. "Bunch of kids."

Mr Smith – that was the second voice! Yes, his accomplice had called him Noah. Maisie stopped fighting, and the other man let her go.

"What are you doing here?" Maisie hissed, as Mr Smith opened a dark lantern much like Jacob's. A soft glow of light lit up their faces, and she saw George and Alice huddled together against the wall of the warehouse.

"Are they coming? Did they hear the dog?" the other man demanded urgently, and Mr Smith peered out.

"No, Dan. They must have just reckoned it was a guard dog. There is one, tied up over by one of the other warehouses."

"Good." The man turned back to look at them and, in the light of the lantern, Maisie saw that he was tall and wore a rough blue jacket, with a spotted handkerchief tied around his neck. He had a cap pulled down low over his eyes, but she could still see that dark red curls were springing out from underneath it. He stared at her and, somehow, his eyes were as familiar as his voice.

"Dad…?" Maisie asked, her own voice very small.

"I didn't think you'd recognize me. I hardly knew you, Maisie. You're so tall."

"It's been years and years," Maisie
whispered.

"This is your dad?" George demanded,
stepping forward. "What did they grab us
for, then?"

"To stop you getting yourselves into

trouble," Mr Smith growled. "We've been watching Miss Eccles and her accomplice. They're nasty."

"How long have you been home?" Maisie asked suddenly. "Why didn't you come and visit us? Gran's desperate to see you!"

"I know, I'm sorry. I wanted to lie low. You have to understand, Maisie – you saw my notes, didn't you? Noah said you got the box."

"And we found your secret pocket," Maisie told him, enjoying the flare of surprise in her father's eyes.

He nodded at her slowly. Admiringly, Maisie realized. She wouldn't tell him that she had only found the pocket by accident – or rather, Eddie had.

"So you know what's at stake here. I wanted to be free to investigate back in London, so I kept my return a secret. But you

142

don't know how I've been longing to come in the back gate and sit down at the kitchen table, Maisie. How much I've been envying Noah. I watched you, a couple of times, you and this other young lady, setting out on your errands with the little dog."

"We didn't spot you," Maisie said, rather indignantly.

Her father chuckled. "Well, perhaps you get your spying skills from me."

"Much as I'm enjoying this touching reunion," Mr Smith muttered, "that lovely pair back there are about to set fire to the ship. We need to fetch the law. They'll have to believe us now."

"You've already been to the police?" Maisie asked.

"They said they couldn't search the docks without more evidence. That's why Noah and

I were hanging around the *Elizabeth Ann*," her father explained.

Mr Smith rubbed his hands together. "They can't say we ain't got enough evidence now, not with Miss Ivy and her mate fetching barrels of brandy. Hey, they're pouring it out, I can smell it."

Maisie sniffed, and almost choked. A rich, sharp smell filled her nose and throat, and for a moment her head swam.

"They must be fair drowning that ship in brandy," George said, coughing a little.

"There's a policeman walking his beat down the Commercial Road. I'd better fetch him," Maisie's father said. "I don't like to leave you here to keep watch, but—"

"They wouldn't believe us," Maisie agreed with a sigh. "They never do."

"I'll be quick," her father promised. "Noah

will stay with you. Take this, just in case, Maisie." He pressed something into her hand – a clasp knife, with an old, well worn leather handle. He made to walk out on to the dock, but then he turned back and swept Maisie into his arms, hugging her tight. "Keep yourself safe. Look after the others," he murmured to her. "I know you will." And he was gone.

Maisie stared after him, her heart thudding. "I will," she whispered. "I promise."

"We'd better get a bit closer. See what those two are doing down there," Mr Smith muttered. "No chat, you hear?"

Maisie and Alice and George glared at him, and Maisie felt like telling Mr Smith that this was *their* mystery.

Quietly, they sneaked out from the little alley between the warehouses and crept back down towards the *Elizabeth Ann,* tied up on the wharf. The smell of brandy grew stronger and stronger, and Alice reeled dizzily against Maisie and George, overcome by the fumes.

"We ain't got time to wait for your dad to come back, Maisie," George whispered urgently, pulling her back a little so that Mr Smith couldn't hear them. "They'll light her up any minute. She's going to go up in seconds, she's that soaked in spirits."

"You mean the evidence will be gone?" Alice gasped. "They won't be caught? The beasts who are robbing Papa?" And she wrenched her arm out of George's and set off at a staggering run towards the gangplank.

"What is she *doing*?" Mr Smith snarled. "They'll see her!"

"She's frightened for her father," Maisie whispered. "Oh, Alice, come back!" she hissed. But Alice didn't turn round, so Maisie raced after her friend. She could hear George muttering furiously as he followed them.

Alice was halfway up the gangplank when Jacob saw her. He had an empty cask under his arm and he was obviously coming to fetch another. He grabbed Alice with one massive hand and dragged her on to the ship.

"Miss Ivy! Miss Ivy!" he growled. "We got a little girl spying about. This the one you was telling me about?"

Miss Eccles appeared hurriedly from a trapdoor leading down under the decks. Her heavy silk frock hissed across the boards with a shhhing sound, and Maisie, dashing up the gangplank after Alice, found herself giving a little shiver of fear.

"There's another one! Behind you!" Miss Eccles shrieked, as Maisie dashed across the deck to snatch at Alice, and Eddie barked and scrabbled at Jacob's tree-trunk legs.

Maisie dragged at the huge man's arm as hard as she could, but he seemed not to feel it. He simply brought his other hand around and swatted her out of the way, as if she were a fly. She rolled across the deck and crawled behind the mast. She felt so dizzy that for a moment all she could think about was how to get away.

Then Jacob did the same to George, who had come racing after them, knocking the butcher's boy hard against the mast that was just in front of Maisie. George hit it with a dreadful thud and he crumpled to the deck like a rag doll. Maisie began to feel sick.

Mr Smith appeared, stomping up the gangplank. Maisie watched him from her place on the deck, half behind the mast, and all she could think of was his rheumatism, and his creaky joints. *Go away!* she begged him silently. *Go! Go away! Don't let him hurt you!*

But Mr Smith came lumbering on, like a gallant old bulldog, and Jacob laughed. He stuffed Alice into Miss Eccles's arms, took one step forward and hit Mr Smith – not even very hard. He didn't really have to try, which made it worse than anything. The old ship's cook folded over with a wheeze.

"Where's the other one?" Miss Eccles snapped, giving Alice a furious shake. "The other little girl?"

"Don't know," Jacob called over, when Alice didn't answer. "Over there somewhere. Doesn't matter, does it. Light the fire. We can take Lacey's brat with us. Lacey would pay to have her back, wouldn't he? He'll pay, and then he'll keep quiet. We'll put the frighteners on him. Tell him we could snatch her again whenever we like."

Miss Eccles looked around for a moment, frowning at George and Mr Smith sprawled on the deck boards, but then she nodded. She reached into the pretty bag she was carrying, and Maisie swallowed a panic-stricken laugh. She had the matches in her nice little bag, the matches she was going to use to set the ship alight, and kill her and George and Mr Smith. It seemed all wrong, that someone so awful should have such a pretty bag...

It's the brandy fumes, Maisie told herself. *And you're frightened. Stop it! You're being stupid and panicking. Think!*

The mast had footholds, Maisie noticed dreamily. Little metal footholds, to help you climb. But what was the point of climbing? The fire would climb, too, and she couldn't carry Eddie up the mast with her, and it wouldn't help George, or Alice or Mr Smith.

"He told me to keep them safe," she whispered, rubbing her aching cheek where Jacob had hit her. "I promised." She looked up and, above her in the rigging, saw a heavy wooden block. Just like the one that was supposed to have fallen from the rigging on the ship in China and knocked out her father. It hadn't been a block, of course. It had been one of Miss Eccles's gang, trying to scare her father off and silence him. Or worse. It hadn't worked, Maisie thought triumphantly. And she wouldn't be scared off either. She wouldn't let them win. She was going to look after her friends.

"Stay, Eddie," she whispered, and the little dog whimpered at her. She patted him and shushed him, and he sank down with his nose on his paws, watching her worriedly.

Maisie began to climb the mast as quietly as she could, feeling the painful drag on her arms as she hauled herself up. Miss Eccles was fiddling with the matches, ready to fling one on to the puddle of spirits they had poured in the middle of the deck. Maisie looked away – Miss Eccles seemed too far down already. Maisie was a city girl, she'd never even climbed a tree. This was like looking over the banisters outside Miss Lane's room, leaning over too far, so her head began to swim. Only a hundred times worse.

"Where *is* that other girl?" Miss Eccles was saying to Jacob, down below. "She couldn't have crept back down the gangplank, could she? What if she's gone for the police? We'd better find her, to make sure."

Any moment now they would look up, Maisie thought. But she was nearly there. The block was just in front of her, fastened on to the rigging.

How was she supposed to loosen the rope, though?

Maisie clung to the mast, staring at the ropes and knots, and wishing she understood how they worked. A breeze ruffled the furled sail, the ropes swung and the mast creaked. She gripped on tighter, feeling the ship move beneath her, and closed her eyes. Her skirts swung, and Maisie felt the heavy weight of the clasp knife thump into her leg. Her father had given her the way to save the others! Maisie pressed her cheek against the smooth wood of the mast and whispered, "Thank you, Dad…"

She drew one hand away from the mast and pulled the knife out of her skirt pocket. She opened it with trembling fingers and began to saw at the rope, her breath hissing with the effort. It seemed to take so long, each strand fraying and separating, and still so many more of them to go. But at last it broke, and the heavy wooden block slid off into her hands.

Jacob was stomping about below her, searching her out. If only he would stand still – just for a moment.

Maisie felt the block slide out of her hands, as though it *wanted* to help her. It struck Jacob on the side of the head, and he teetered and slowly dropped like a felled tree.

Miss Eccles screamed and let go of Alice. Still holding the lighted match, she turned to look up at Maisie. The yellow flame lit her face eerily, and Maisie shivered. She had never seen anyone look so angry…

And then Maisie heard a thundering of footsteps and a stream of policemen ran up the gangplank, with Maisie's father at the front. As she edged her way down the mast, there was a clamour of voices below her.

"Stop right there!"

"Maisie, Maisie, where are you?"

Tower Bridge, a week later

"You're going to stay, then?" Maisie murmured, leaning over the rail and staring at the river swirling below them. Tower Bridge was the closest crossing over the river to the docks, and she could see the forest of masts. The wind changed a little, and Maisie could swear she caught a whiff of brandy.

"Mmm-hmm," said her father. "I was tired of life at sea. Never in one place long enough. But I didn't ever think I could do anything else." Her father brushed his red hair out of his eyes.

Maisie glanced up at him. "What *are* you going to do now?"

Her father smiled at her and dug into his jacket pocket. He was wearing a smart brown tweed suit and he didn't look like a scruffy sailor any more. "I'm going to do what I've been doing for the last few months, Maisie. Only hopefully, people might pay me for it." He pulled out a little leather card case, and handed Maisie a card.

"Hitchins and Hitchins," she read, frowning. "Private Inquiry Agents… Discreet Inquiries in England or Abroad. Apply at 31 Albion Street, London." The card was beautiful – creamy white, with the type neat and small.

A Detective Agency! Her own father, a proper consulting detective, like her hero Gilbert Carrington! And as for the other Hitchins… Maisie blushed proudly.

"I put an advertisement in all the papers, as well. Your gran says we can use the lodgers' sitting room as our office and consulting room," her father explained. "No one ever sits in it anyway, she says." He put his hand over hers. "So will you be my partner, Maisie? You've solved more cases than I have. And that Inspector Grange, the one who arrested Miss Ivy, told me that you were a meddling little busybody who couldn't keep her nose out. But then he grudgingly mentioned that occasionally you had been quite useful…"

"Quite useful!" Maisie squeaked indignantly, and Eddie let out a sharp little bark. "I caught a whole gang of ruthless art thieves for him!"

"He did admit that you had something to do with that one," her father agreed. "Although he said that he was close behind you all the time."

Maisie rolled her eyes. "So … I don't have to go back to school? Gran said maybe I should, when you came home."

"The professor wants to lend you books to read and talk to you about them," her father explained. "He told me you were extremely intelligent. I'm sure you'd learn more from him than you would at school, to be honest."

"Will you come and live at the house

as well?" Maisie asked hopefully. "Oh … I suppose there isn't the space. If Alice wasn't with us, I could sleep with Gran and you could have my room. We telegraphed her father at all the ports where the ship will put in. They'll be back in a few weeks, I'm sure."

"That's all right, I'll be taking Noah's rooms in a day or so. He's missing the sea."

"But his rheumatism!" Maisie shook her head. "I don't think he ought to go back to working on a ship." Mr Smith had recovered from being knocked out, but Maisie was sure he was looking older and more fragile than he had before.

Her father laughed. "He's going to live in Brighton and run his own lodging house. He says he's learned a lot from watching your gran, and he's got a nest egg saved up to buy a house near the sea. He says

London's too dangerous. He wants a quiet life, he told me." Daniel Hitchins looked worriedly at Maisie. "Would you rather go back to school? Are you tired of detecting?"

"Of course not!"

"You don't think I'm stealing your thunder?"

Maisie beamed at him. "No. After all, I must have got the detecting from somewhere, mustn't I? Gran always said you were terribly nosy as a little boy."

Her father grinned. "I suppose I was. But I wanted to travel. I was curious about everything, that's why I went to sea."

"*Discreet Inquiries in England or Abroad…*" Maisie repeated.

"Exactly. After all, my first mystery started in China. And wouldn't you like to see the world, Maisie?"

Maisie gazed down the river at the lines of

masts. An excited laugh bubbled inside her, and suddenly she threw her arms around her father's waist – the first time she had hugged him since that night at the docks.

"I would," she told him. "I really would."

Collect the whole series

The Case of the Stolen Sixpence

When Maisie rescues an abandoned puppy, he quickly leads her to her first case. George, the butcher's boy, has been sacked for stealing, but Maisie's sure he's innocent. It's time for Maisie to put her detective skills to the test as she follows the trail of the missing money…

The Case of the Vanishing Emerald

When star-of-the-stage Sarah Massey comes to visit, Maisie senses a mystery. Sarah is distraught – her fiancé has given her a priceless emerald necklace and now it's gone missing. Maisie sets out to investigate, but nothing is what it seems in the theatrical world of make-believe…

The Case of the
Phantom Cat

Maisie has been invited to the country as a
companion for her best friend, Alice. But as soon
as the girls arrive, they are warned that the manor
house they're staying in is haunted. With Alice
terrified by the strange goings-on, it's up to Maisie
to prove there's no such thing as ghosts…

The Case of the Feathered Mask

Maisie loves to look at the amazing objects her friend Professor Tobin has collected on his travels around the world. But when a thief steals a rare and valuable wooden mask, leaving only a feather behind, Maisie realizes she has a new mystery on her hands…

The Case of the Secret Tunnel

Gran has a new lodger and Maisie suspects there's more to him than meets the eye. Fred Grange says he works for a biscuit company, but he is out at odd hours and knows nothing about biscuits! Determined to uncover the truth, Maisie is drawn into a mystery that takes her deep underground…

The Case of the Spilled Ink

Alice has gone missing from her new boarding school, and it's up to Maisie to track her down before she ends up in real danger. Maisie suspects there is more to her friend's disappearance than there first seems. But her only clues are an inkwell spilled across Alice's desk and a trail of paw prints...

The Case of the Blind Beetle

Lord Dacre, an old friend of Professor Tobin, has had his greatest treasure stolen – an ancient Egyptian scarab beetle. What's more, someone is sending him threatening messages, and there is talk of a pharaoh's curse… Can Maisie get to the bottom of the mystery and find the thief?

Maisie Hitchins
The Case of the Stolen Sixpence

HOLLY WEBB

Maisie Hitchins
The Case of the Vanishing Emerald

HOLLY WEBB

Maisie Hitchins
The Case of the Phantom Cat

HOLLY WEBB

Maisie Hitchins
The Case of the Feathered Mask

HOLLY WEBB

Maisie Hitchins
The Case of the Secret Tunnel

HOLLY WEBB

Maisie Hitchins
The Case of the Spilled Ink

HOLLY WEBB

Maisie Hitchins
The Case of the Blind Beetle

HOLLY WEBB

Maisie Hitchins
The Case of the Weeping Mermaid

HOLLY WEBB

Find out more about Holly Webb

www.holly-webb.com